Printed in the United States of America

1 3 5 7 9 10 8 6 4 2

Library of Congress Catalog Card Number on file.

ISBN: 1-4231-0597-4

Walt Disney's
ALICE in WONDERLAND

Adapted from the film by
Teddy Slater

Illustrated by
Holly Hannon
and
Franc Mateu

Disney PRESS
New York

Chapter One

One golden spring day, a young girl named Alice sat perched in a tree listening to her big sister read aloud from a history book. At least, that's what she was supposed to be doing. In fact, she was idly weaving a daisy chain for her cat, Dinah, who was curled up beside her on the sturdy low branch.

As her sister's soft voice droned on, Alice dangled one white-stockinged leg over the branch. A black, foot-shaped shadow swung across the page.

"Alice!" the older girl cried. "Will you kindly pay attention to your history lesson?"

Alice peered down at her sister, who was leaning against the tree trunk. A big boring schoolbook was propped open in her lap. "I'm sorry," said Alice, stifling a yawn, "but how can one possibly pay attention to a book that has no pictures?"

"My dear child," Alice's sister replied, "there are a great many good books in this world without pictures."

"In this world, perhaps," Alice said dreamily, "but in my world, the books would be nothing *but* pictures."

"Your world!" her sister scoffed, turning back to her book. "What nonsense!"

"Nonsense . . . ," Alice echoed thoughtfully.

"That's it, Dinah!" Alice exclaimed suddenly, scooping up the

1

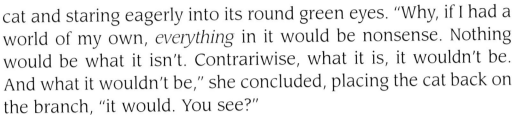

cat and staring eagerly into its round green eyes. "Why, if I had a world of my own, *everything* in it would be nonsense. Nothing would be what it isn't. Contrariwise, what it is, it wouldn't be. And what it wouldn't be," she concluded, placing the cat back on the branch, "it would. You see?"

"Meow," Dinah replied as Alice climbed gracefully down from the tree.

"In my world," Alice said, looking up at Dinah, "you wouldn't say 'Meow.' You'd say, 'Yes, Miss Alice.' "

"Meow," Dinah repeated.

"Oh, but you would," Alice insisted, reaching up and pulling the cat down from the tree. "You'd be just like people, Dinah, and so would all the other animals."

Alice set Dinah gently on the riverbank and continued her daydream. "In my world," she declared, "cats and rabbits would live in fancy little houses and be dressed in shoes and hats and trousers."

Dropping to the ground beside Dinah, Alice gazed wistfully into the gently flowing water. But even as she tried to imagine a wonderland of her own making, her voice slowly trailed off and her eyelids fluttered shut.

Chapter Two

"Meow! Meow! Meow!"

Alice's eyes snapped open just in time to see a large white rabbit hopping from rock to rock across the river.

"Meow! Meow!" Dinah cried again, racing back and forth along the riverbank.

"Hush, Dinah," Alice chided. "It's only a rabbit."

And so it was.

But this was no ordinary rabbit. For one thing, he was wearing a most extraordinary waistcoat. For another, he was holding an oversize gold pocketwatch in one furry paw, and he seemed to be in a most awful hurry.

"Oh, my fur and whiskers," fretted the White Rabbit as he hopped from a rock onto the opposite bank. "I'm late!"

Alice watched him scamper off. "Now, that's curious," she mused, a puzzled frown on her face. "What could a rabbit possibly be late for? Well, whatever it is," she decided, "it must be awfully important. Perhaps it's a party. Wait, Mister Rabbit!" Alice called out. "Wait!"

But the White Rabbit had no time for idle chitchat. "I'm late!" he muttered. "I'm late! I'm late!"

Alice caught up to the White Rabbit just as he disappeared into a hole in the ground.

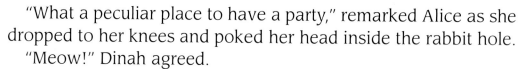

"What a peculiar place to have a party," remarked Alice as she dropped to her knees and poked her head inside the rabbit hole.

"Meow!" Dinah agreed.

Alice pushed and squeezed her way through the narrow opening. "You know, Dinah," she said, "we really shouldn't be doing this. After all, we haven't been invited. And curiosity often leads to . . . troublllle. . . ."

Alice barely had time to wave good-bye to Dinah before she found herself falling head over heels down the rabbit hole.

Down, down, down Alice plummeted. She was feeling quite uneasy when suddenly her long skirt caught the air like a big blue parachute, and she floated slowly down the rest of the way.

Alice landed just in time to see the White Rabbit race down a shadowy corridor.

"Oh, Mister Rabbit," she called, racing after him. "Wait! Please!" But the White Rabbit had already disappeared behind a big green door.

Alice pulled open the door—only to find another, smaller door behind it. And behind *that* door was a third, even smaller door. And so it went. The last door was so small that Alice could barely crawl through the opening. But after pushing and pushing she finally made it to the other side.

Alice found herself in a large, empty room with a high ceiling. There was no sign of the White Rabbit, but there was, however, one tiny door on the far side of the room.

"Curiouser and curiouser," murmured Alice as she marched across the room and turned the shiny brass doorknob.

"Ouch!" said the Doorknob.

"Oh! I beg your pardon!" Alice gasped, snatching back her hand. On closer inspection Alice discovered that the shiny brass knob was really a shiny brass *nose*!

6

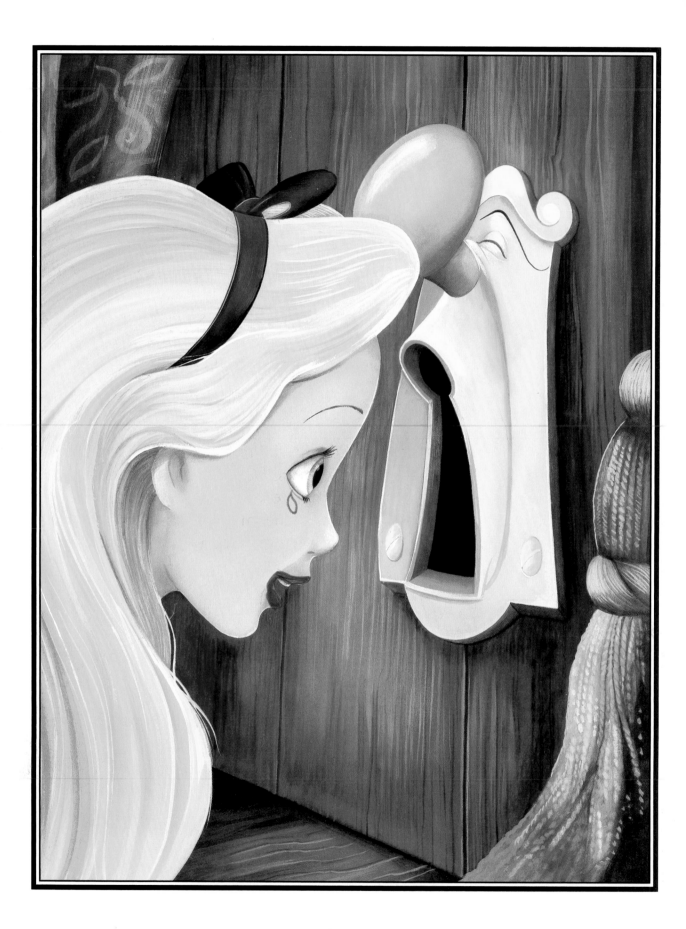

"It's quite all right," the Doorknob assured Alice. "But you did give me quite a turn."

"You see," Alice began, "I was following—"

"Ha! Ha! Ha!" laughed the Doorknob. "Doorknob . . . turn. Get it?" Then he burst out laughing again.

"Please, sir," Alice said impatiently. "I'm looking for a white rabbit. So, if you don't mind . . ." Alice bent down to peek through the keyhole, which was actually the Doorknob's mouth.

"One good turn deserves another," said the Doorknob agreeably. And with that, the Doorknob opened the keyhole wide enough to give Alice a good look into the room beyond.

"There he is!" exclaimed Alice as she caught sight of the rabbit. "I simply must get through."

"Sorry," the Doorknob said. "You're much too big. Simply impassable."

"You mean impossible," Alice corrected him.

"No," the Doorknob repeated, "*impassable*. Nothing's impossible," he declared. "Why don't you try the bottle on the table?"

"What table?" asked Alice just as one magically appeared beside her. On the table was a sparkling glass bottle with a tag marked Drink Me!

"Just follow the directions," said the Doorknob, "and directly you'll be directed in the right direction."

Alice popped off the cork and gave the bottle a cautious sniff. What if it held poison? Alice had to consider. But once more, curiosity got the better of her. She put the bottle to her mouth and took a drink.

"Hmm . . . ," Alice said, licking her lips. "It tastes like a cherry tart. No," she said, after a second sip, "more like custard."

By the time she'd decided what it *really* tasted like—"Roast turkey, for goodness' sake!"—the bottle was nearly empty! It also

seemed to have grown. At least, that's what Alice decided, for the bottle was now a great deal bigger than she was. But the bottle hadn't changed, Alice was amazed to discover. It was she who, quite clearly, had shrunk!

"Look!" cried Alice, now eyeball to eyeball with the Doorknob. "I'm just the right size!"

When Alice reached out and turned the knob, however, the Doorknob laughed again. "I forgot to tell you," he said. "I'm locked! Ha! Ha!"

"Oh no!" Alice cried, not at all amused.

"But don't worry," the Doorknob told her between giggles. "You've got the key."

"What key?" asked Alice.

"Now don't tell me you left it up . . . there," the Doorknob said.

Alice looked up . . . and up . . . and up. Her eyes widened in amazement when a brass key suddenly appeared from out of nowhere on the table.

Alice gave a sigh. She was just the right size to fit through the door, but now she was much too small to reach up to the table for the key.

"Whatever will I do?" she wailed.

"Try that," suggested the Doorknob. A small cardboard box marked Eat Me materialized at Alice's feet.

Alice stared curiously at the box for just a moment, then reached inside, pulled out a cookie, and took a bite. She had barely finished chewing before she shot up and was back to her normal size! But when she swallowed, she shot up again. Now she was quite abnormally tall. In fact, she didn't stop growing until her head bumped the ceiling.

"I must say," the Doorknob remarked. "A little of that went a long way. Ha! Ha! Ha!"

"Well, I don't think it's so funny," Alice said. "Now I shall never get out!"

"Oh, come now," said the Doorknob as two huge teardrops rolled down Alice's cheeks and splashed onto the floor. "Crying won't help."

"I know," sobbed Alice, "but I can't seem to stop it."

The floor quickly became flooded in a pool of tears! The Doorknob watched nervously as the water level climbed higher and higher.

"This won't do at all," he spluttered through a great mouthful of salt water. "You up there," he shouted at Alice, *"stop!"*

Just then Alice noticed the glass bottle floating in the water. With one giant hand, she reached out and grabbed it.

No sooner had Alice taken a drink than she began to shrink again. She grew smaller and smaller until she was so small that she could climb inside the bottle.

"I do wish I hadn't cried so much," sighed Alice as she bobbed along on a sea of her own tears. She sailed through the keyhole and into a world of wonder.

Chapter Three

From inside the bottle, Alice looked out onto a vast, empty ocean. As far as she could see it was all gray fog and cold blue water.

Suddenly, from out of the fog, Alice heard a hearty voice belting out a sea chantey:

Oh, a sailor's life is the life for me.
How I love to sail o'er the bounding sea.

A moment later the singer sailed into view. Alice was astonished, for he was, in fact, a large, cheerful-looking dodo bird. He was rather well dressed, Alice thought, and clearly in command of his vessel. Actually, it was the vessel itself that most attracted Alice's interest. For the Dodo was perched not on the deck of a ship but on the upended feet of a toucan, who was skimming across the water on his beak. Alice noticed that an enormous blue eagle was propelling them along by flapping his wings at the Dodo's back.

Alice gaped in amazement as the Dodo broke off his song and cried, "Land ho, by Jove! Three points to starboard! Pull away, me hearties!"

"Oh, Mr. Dodo!" Alice cried. "Please help me!" But the Dodo and his friends had already vanished back into the fog.

Not long after, another most astonishing trio of birds appeared bobbing along the water on a log. This time it was a pelican, an owl, and a parrot.

"Yoo-hoo!" Alice called out to them, but the birds paid her no mind. Nor did the lobsters who rowed past her next, using their bright red claws as oars.

Alice poked her head out of the bottle just as a giant wave loomed behind her. "Help!" she cried as the great wave crashed over her. *Whoosh!* Alice suddenly was lifted up out of the bottle by the great wave, only to be dragged down to the sandy bottom of the sea. Finally, drenched and miserable, Alice was greatly relieved to find herself tossed up onshore.

Alice lay in a heap on the sand, trying to catch her breath. But that was easier said than done, for each time Alice lifted her head, it was roughly pushed back into the sand by someone running over her!

Alice decided she had had quite enough when she recognized the familiar booming voice of the Dodo. He was sitting on a rock shouting orders:

Forward, backward, inward, outward,
   Come and join the chase.
Nothing could be drier
   Than a jolly caucus race.

The Dodo's feathered friends were dashing around him in a big circle, skipping, flapping, and fluttering, all in an attempt to dry off. But each time a wave crashed onshore, everyone but the Dodo got drenched.

It made no sense to Alice, but the Dodo soon had her running in circles, too. She had barely run around once when the White Rabbit washed up on the beach. He was still carrying his pocketwatch and still muttering, "I'm late, I'm late, I'm late!"

As the rabbit hopped over the sand, Alice dropped out of the Dodo's silly race and ran after the White Rabbit. But once again he was too fast for her. Alice followed the rabbit's paw prints across the sand, but the trail ended at a grove of trees

16

by the edge of the beach.

Alice was still searching for the White Rabbit when she came upon two roly-poly fellows standing still as stones between two trees. They were wearing identical red beanies, red trousers, and big blue bow ties. The only difference between them was the writing on their shirt collars: one read Tweedledee, the other Tweedledum.

"What peculiar little statues," mused Alice as she studied them intently. Then she playfully poked one in the belly.

Only then did Alice realize her mistake. The two weren't statues at all. In fact, they were very much alive.

"If you think we're waxworks, you ought to pay, you know," scolded the one labeled Tweedledee.

"Contrariwise," said Tweedledum, "if you think we're alive, you ought to speak to us."

Before Alice could utter a word, Tweedledee and Tweedledum began an odd little dance. Alice waited, a trifle impatiently, until they were finished. Then she curtsied politely and said good-bye.

"You're beginning backward," protested Tweedledee as he ran ahead of Alice and blocked her way.

"Yes," agreed Tweedledum when he appeared beside his brother. "The first thing in a visit is to state your name and business. Then shake hands, shake hands, shake hands."

To illustrate, Tweedledee and Tweedledum each took one of Alice's hands and pumped it up and down. "That's manners!" the tubby twosome chorused, shaking Alice right off her feet and onto the ground.

"Really!" sniffed Alice as she picked herself up and smoothed down her skirts. Then, turning to go, she said, "My name is Alice, and I'm following the White Rabbit, so—"

"Oh, you can't leave yet," said Tweedledum, once again blocking her way.

17

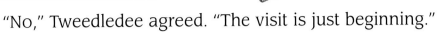

"No," Tweedledee agreed. "The visit is just beginning."

But Alice had already had quite enough of their foolishness. "I really must be going," she insisted, brushing past the twins. "I'm curious to know where the White Rabbit is going."

"Ohhh," Tweedledum exclaimed, winking at his brother behind Alice's back. "She's curious."

"The oysters were curious, too," remarked Tweedledee, just loud enough for Alice to hear. "And look what happened to them, poor things."

"Tsk! Tsk!" said the two dramatically.

Poor Alice! She really did want to know what the rabbit was up to, but she was now awfully curious about what had happened to the oysters. She hesitated a moment and then turned back to the twins. "What *did* happen to the oysters?" she asked.

"Oh, you wouldn't be interested," Tweedledee said coyly. But clearly Alice was.

Chapter Four

As soon as Alice was seated comfortably on a log, Tweedledee announced: " 'The Walrus and the Carpenter' . . ."

"Or, 'The Story of the Curious Oysters,'" Tweedledum chimed in. Then he cleared his throat and began to recite:

The Walrus and the Carpenter
  Were walking close at hand;
The beach was wide from side to side
  But much too full of sand.
"Mr. Walrus," said the Carpenter,
  "My brain begins to perk.
We'll sweep this clear in half a year,
  If you don't mind the work."

But as it turned out, the Walrus most definitely did mind.

"The time has come," the Walrus said,
  "To talk of other things:
Of shoes—and ships—and sealing wax—
  And cabbages—and kings—
And why the sea is boiling hot—
  And whether pigs have wings.
Calloo, callay, no work today!
  We're cabbages and kings."

Alice was quite enjoying the story, though she was beginning to wonder what, if anything, it had to do with oysters. Finally, it all became clear.

It seems that the Walrus and the Carpenter were strolling along the beach one day when they spied a bed of oysters in a pool under several feet of water. While the Carpenter watched

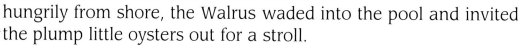

hungrily from shore, the Walrus waded into the pool and invited the plump little oysters out for a stroll.

Their mother warned them not to go, but the little oysters were curious about the world above the sea. So they followed the Walrus onto the shore, across the sand, and into a ramshackle seafood restaurant the Carpenter had hastily hammered together.

Of course, when the Walrus slyly suggested dinner, the oysters had no way of knowing just what—or who—he had in mind. They joined him at a table and waited trustingly while the Walrus sent the Carpenter out to the kitchen for a loaf of bread.

Not five minutes passed before the Carpenter returned, ready to partake of the feast. But it was too late, for all that remained was an enormous pile of empty oystershells. And a very stuffed Walrus! As Tweedledee so poetically summed it up:

"Little oysters!" cried the Carpenter.
    But answer came there none—
And that was scarcely odd 'cause they'd
    Been eaten . . . every one!

"The end!" Tweedledum informed Alice proudly.

"That was a very sad story," said Alice, deeply moved. "But I really must be going now," she said, getting up from the log. "It's been a very nice visit."

But the twins still weren't ready to lose their audience.

"Another recitation," cried Tweedledee, pushing Alice back onto the log. "This one's entitled 'Father William.' " Before she could protest, he began:

"You are old, Father William," the young man said,
    "And your hair has become very white;
And yet you incessantly stand on your head—
    Do you think, at your age, it is right?"

While Tweedledee was still reciting, and while Tweedledum was busy standing on his head, Alice took the opportunity to slip softly away.

Chapter Five

A short time later, on the other side of the woods, Alice came upon a little white cottage with a pretty pink door and shutters. "Now, I wonder who lives here?" she asked herself.

Suddenly the shutters on the upstairs window flew open and out popped the White Rabbit. "Mary Ann! Mary Ann!" he called out. "Drat that girl!" he muttered. Then he pulled his head back inside the window and slammed the shutters closed.

A moment later the White Rabbit came rushing out of the house. He was wearing a short white tunic with a stiff round collar, and along with his pocketwatch he carried a trumpet.

"Excuse me," Alice said as he ran past her. "I've been trying—"

At the sound of Alice's voice, the White Rabbit stopped, turned, and peered at Alice through his spectacles. "Why, Mary Ann!" he cried in a scolding tone. "What are you doing out here?"

"Mary Ann?" said Alice.

"Well, don't just stand there," said the White Rabbit, hopping up and down. "I'm late. Go get my gloves, Mary Ann."

"But I'm not—," Alice began, but the White Rabbit shooed her toward the house.

"My gloves!" he shouted. "At once!" And he seemed so upset that Alice decided it was best not to argue.

Alice wandered into the cottage and climbed up a flight of

stairs to the rabbit's bedroom. "Now, let me see," she murmured, gazing around the cozy little room. "If I were a rabbit, where would I keep my gloves?"

A jar on the bureau caught her eye. But there were no gloves inside it, just a batch of cookies. Suddenly feeling very hungry, Alice reached into the jar and took one. And since the words Eat Me were scrawled across the cookie in pink icing, that's just what Alice did.

"Oh no!" Alice exclaimed. Suddenly she felt herself growing again. She grew and grew and grew until she was much too big for the little room.

Meanwhile, the White Rabbit was waiting outside for his gloves. Losing his patience at last, he stomped back into the house. "See here, Mary Ann," he grumbled.

The White Rabbit was only halfway up the stairs when a huge white-stockinged foot burst through his bedroom door and knocked him tumbling back down.

"H-E-L-P!" screamed the White Rabbit as the huge foot grew even huger. And before he knew what had hit him, he was knocked outside, where he landed—*splat!*—flat on his back.

By the time the White Rabbit picked himself up, Alice's enormous foot was sticking out through the front door. And sticking out through the windows were another foot—just as huge—and two enormously long arms.

"Oh dear!" sighed Alice from inside the house, where the rest of her was firmly wedged. But the White Rabbit didn't hear her. He was racing down the street, crying, "Help! Monster!"

The rabbit returned in short order, accompanied by the Dodo. "Oh, my poor little bitty house," Alice heard the White Rabbit moan. "Oh, my roof and rafters. Oh, my walls and—"

"Steady, old chap," said the Dodo. "Mustn't go all to pieces."

"Well, do something," the rabbit demanded tearfully.

"Yes indeed," said the Dodo as he studied the house from top to bottom. "Extraordinary situation, but—"

"But what?" asked the White Rabbit.

"But I have a very simple solution," said the Dodo. "Simply pull the monster out the chimney."

That seemed to make sense to the White Rabbit. "Go on," he said, pushing the Dodo toward the house. "Pull it out!"

"Who, me?" said the Dodo, digging in his heels. "Don't be ridiculous! What we need is a . . . uh . . . uh . . ." The Dodo's voice trailed off as a green lizard dressed as a chimney sweep came walking down the street. "What we need is a lizard with a ladder!" proclaimed the Dodo triumphantly.

"Oh, Bill! Bill!" the White Rabbit called out, waving the chimney sweep in through the gate. "C-c-can you help us? We need a lazard with a lizard. I mean a liddered with a—"

"At your service, gov'nor," said the lizard, grinning toothily. And since the lizard seemed so agreeable, the Dodo thought there would be no harm in asking.

"Bill," the Dodo asked, "could you just pop down the chimney and send that monster out of there?"

"Righto," Bill said confidently. Without further ado, he leaned his ladder against the house and scrambled up to the upstairs window. Bill, however, quickly began to have second thoughts. He took one look at Alice's big blue eye staring out at him, shrieked, *"Monster!"* and scrambled down the ladder as fast as his four legs could carry him.

It took more than a bit of coaxing, but the Dodo finally managed to get Bill back up the ladder to the chimney. "Nothing to it, old boy," he insisted. "Simply tie your tail around the monster's head and drag it out." He stuffed Bill's long green tail down the chimney.

28

"But, but, but," protested Bill to no avail. With a hearty "Good luck," the Dodo gave Bill one big push, and the lizard went tumbling down the chimney in a black cloud of soot.

Inside the house, Alice's nose began to twitch as the soot settled over her.

"Ah . . . ah . . . ah . . . CHOO!" Alice's sneeze blasted Bill back up the chimney and into the clear blue sky.

"Perhaps we should try a more energetic remedy," the Dodo remarked as he watched Bill sailing away toward the horizon.

"Anything, anything," pleaded the White Rabbit. "But hurry. I'm late!"

"Well then," said the Dodo, "I propose we burn the house down!" Before the White Rabbit could object, the Dodo began dragging all the White Rabbit's furniture from the house.

"Oh, my poor furniture!" cried the White Rabbit when the Dodo began to smash it up for kindling. "Oh, my poor house," he blubbered as the Dodo searched his pockets for a match.

"Oh my!" sighed Alice when she realized what was about to happen. "This *is* serious."

Alice searched in vain for a way out. Suddenly, she caught sight of the White Rabbit's garden. "Perhaps if I ate something," she reasoned, reaching for a ripe carrot, "it would make me grow smaller."

But the White Rabbit, who had already seen the Dodo destroy a great deal of his prized furniture and was on the verge of seeing his cherished house go up in flames, was at the very least determined to save his vegetable patch. Before Alice could pluck the carrot from the ground, the White Rabbit grabbed hold of it and held on with all his might.

"Let go!" he demanded as Alice pulled the carrot *and* the White Rabbit in through the window.

30

"I'm sorry," Alice said sincerely, "but I must eat something."

"Not *me*, you . . . you . . . you . . . barbarian!" the White Rabbit sputtered, shrinking fearfully away from Alice's enormous teeth. But he needn't have worried, for Alice took one dainty bite of the carrot and immediately began to shrink. She shrank and she shrank and she shrank. . . .

Chapter Six

By the time Alice stopped shrinking, she was no bigger than a mouse, and the White Rabbit was off and running again.

"Wait, Mister Rabbit!" Alice cried, but he was already bounding down the stairs and out the door. Alice hurried after him, as fast as her little legs could carry her.

"Oh dear," sighed Alice as she followed the White Rabbit into the woods. "I'll never catch him while I'm this small." Indeed, the White Rabbit was no longer in sight.

Alice was wondering what to do next when a most unusual insect flitted by. If Alice didn't know better, she'd have sworn its wings were made of dough.

"What a curious-looking butterfly," she said aloud.

"You mean *bread*-and-butterfly," came a voice.

"Oh yes, of course," Alice replied, looking around to see who had spoken. All that she saw, however, was a bed of gaily colored flowers. Then her gaze fell on yet another, even more curious-looking insect.

"Why, it's a horsefly," Alice concluded. "I mean a *rocking*-horsefly." For indeed, the little insect was rocking back and forth in front of her face, whinnying softly, just as a real horse might.

"Naturally," came the voice again. This time, when Alice turned around she found a tall red rose staring back at her.

"I beg your pardon," began Alice, "but, did you . . . ?" Alice's voice trailed off as she studied the rose more carefully. Then she shook her head. "But that's nonsense," she told herself. "Flowers can't talk."

"Of course we can talk," said the rose quite clearly.

"*If* there's anyone worth talking to," said a snooty iris.

"We sing, too," chorused the pansies. With that, all the flowers put their heads together and burst into song.

When the flowers were finished, Alice clapped her hands together and said, "Oh, that was lovely."

"Thank you, my dear," said the rose, bowing modestly.

The other flowers stared at Alice curiously. Finally, a fluffy white daisy asked Alice, "And what garden do *you* come from?"

"I don't come from any garden," replied Alice.

The daisy turned to the iris and gasped. "Do you suppose she's a wildflower?" she asked.

"Oh no," Alice giggled. "I'm not a wildflower."

"Then just what species—or shall we say genus—are you?" the rose asked haughtily.

"Well," Alice said, giving the question some thought. "I suppose you'd call me a genus *Humanus . . . alice.*"

"Hmpf!" The daisy took a long look at Alice's full blue skirt, then bent her head confidentially toward the iris. "Did you ever see an alice with a blossom like that?" she sneered.

"Come to think of it," sniffed the iris, "did you ever see an alice?"

"And did you notice her petals?" jeered the daisy, taking a closer look at Alice's blond hair. "What a peculiar color!"

"And no fragrance," the iris chimed in, bending her head to sniff Alice's hair.

"Ha! Ha!" tittered the daisy rudely as she pulled Alice's skirt

away from her legs. "Just look at those stems."

"Rather scrawny, I'd say," the iris said cattily.

"Well, I think she's pretty," a sweet little rosebud said. But a green leaf clapped itself over the little flower's mouth. "Quiet, bud!" the leaf snapped.

"But I'm not a flower!" protested Alice.

"Aha!" gloated the iris. "Just as I suspected. She's nothing but a common *Mobile vulgaris*."

"A common what?" Alice demanded.

"To put it bluntly," the iris replied, "a weed!"

"I am not a weed!" Alice said indignantly.

"Well, you wouldn't expect her to admit it," one tulip gossiped to another.

"Can you imagine!" said the lilac.

"The nerve of her!" exclaimed the daisy.

"Don't let her stay here and go to seed," warned the lily.

"Go on now," the flowers yelled at Alice, pushing her roughly out of the garden. "We don't want any weeds here."

"Oh, all right," Alice muttered, "if that's the way you feel about it. But if I was my right size," she said huffily, "I could pick every one of you. I guess that'd teach you!"

As she walked away, Alice decided that at the very least the flowers in Wonderland had a lot to learn—especially when it came to manners.

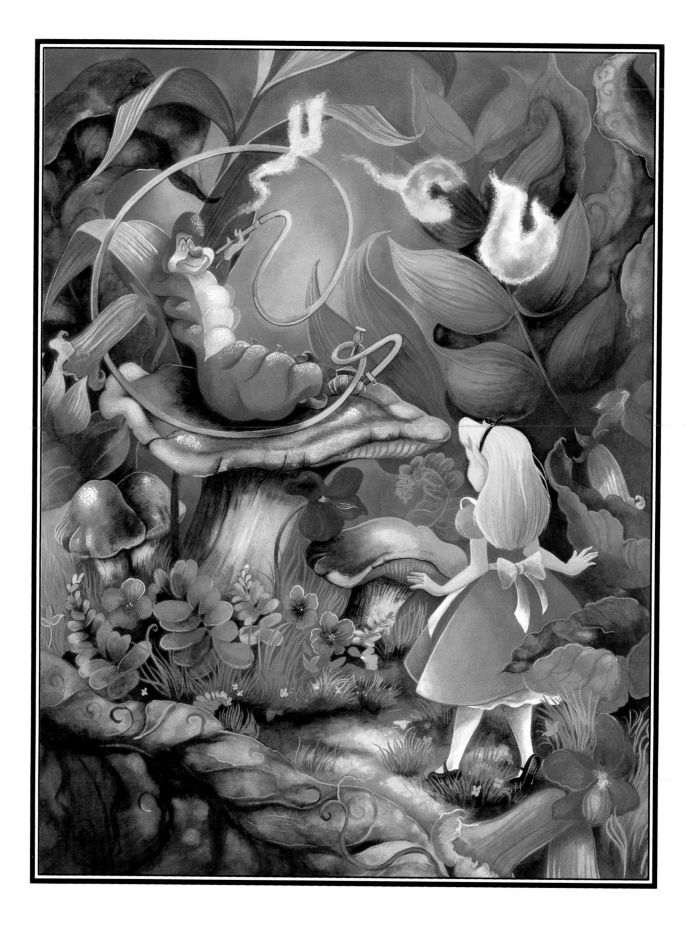

Chapter Seven

The flowers' taunts were still ringing in her ears as Alice continued on her way. But suddenly she heard another sound—a strange voice slowly chanting, "A . . . E . . . I . . . O . . . U! A . . . E . . . I . . . O . . . U! O . . . U . . . E . . . I . . . O! A . . . U . . . E . . . A . . . A!"

Alice followed the chanting to a giant mushroom, where a big blue caterpillar sat smoking a water pipe. On his feet (all six of them) were six golden slippers. And on his face was a sleepy smile.

Alice stared up at him, and the Caterpillar took a puff from his pipe. "Who . . . are . . . youuuuu?" he asked, and he blew a U-shaped smoke ring right in her face.

"Why, I hardly know, sir," replied Alice politely. "I've changed so many times this morning, you see."

"Nooo, I do not see," said the Caterpillar. He sent a smoky C into the air to emphasize his point. "Explain yourself."

"I'm afraid I can't explain myself," Alice told him truthfully, "because I'm not myself, you know."

"Nooo, I do not know," said the Caterpillar, folding his arms (all six of them) across his chest and staring down at her sternly.

"Well," Alice said, "I can't put it any more clearly, for it isn't clear to me."

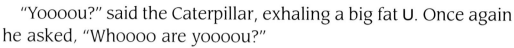

"Yoooou?" said the Caterpillar, exhaling a big fat **U**. Once again he asked, "Whoooo are yoooou?"

"Well," Alice said, choking on all the smoke, "don't you think you ought to tell me who you are first?"

The Caterpillar took another puff on his pipe before answering. At last he said, "Whyyyy?" Only it came out like the letter **Y**.

"Oh dear," sighed Alice, plopping herself down on a toadstool. "Everything is so confusing."

"Whyyyy?" the Caterpillar repeated with another smoky **Y**.

"Well, I can't remember things as I used to," Alice said, "and—"

"Recite!" demanded the Caterpillar, interrupting Alice's explanation. Alice, who'd been quite good at memorizing her lessons at school, jumped to her feet and dutifully began reciting a familiar poem.

> *How doth the little busy bee*
>   *Improve each shi—*

"Stop!" cried the Caterpillar, waving his arms in disgust. "That is not spoken cor-rec-tic-al-ly," he enunciated slowly. "It goes:

> *How doth the little crocodile*
>   *Improve his shining tail,*
> *And pour the waters of the Nile*
>   *On every golden scale.*
>
> *How cheerfully he seems to grin,*
>   *How neatly spread his claws,*
> *And welcome little fishes in*
>   *With gently smiling jaws!"*

Upon concluding the poem, the Caterpillar bowed to Alice, obviously expecting to be greeted with an enthusiastic round of applause.

"I must say," Alice said diplomatically, "I've never heard it that way before."

The Caterpillar sent a thick cloud of smoke in Alice's direction before replying. "I know," he said smugly. "I have improved it."

It took a while for Alice to stop coughing and catch her breath. "Well," she finally sputtered, "if you ask me—"

"Yoooou?" the Caterpillar said, as if he'd never seen her before. "Whoooo are yoooou?"

It was clear to Alice that this conversation was going nowhere. Pushing her way angrily through the smoke, she turned and marched off into the woods.

"You there!" the Caterpillar called after her. "Wait! I have something important to say!"

Alice, who by now probably should have known better, couldn't help wondering what it might be that the Caterpillar had to say. She walked back to the mushroom, where the Caterpillar was now lying on his back, lazily puffing his pipe.

Alice gazed coldly up at the Caterpillar. "Well?" she demanded.

The Caterpillar calmly exhaled a ring or two of smoke before he lazily replied, "Keep your temper."

"Is that all?" snapped Alice.

"No," said the Caterpillar, rolling over and slowly climbing to his feet. "Ex-ac-tic-al-ly what," he asked after a long, smoky pause, "is your problem?"

"Well," Alice said, "it's exactic . . . exactic . . . well, it's precisely this: I should like to be a little larger, sir."

"Why?" the Caterpillar wanted to know.

"Well, three inches is such a wretched height," Alice remarked.

41

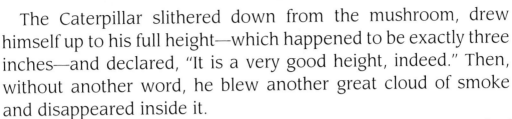

The Caterpillar slithered down from the mushroom, drew himself up to his full height—which happened to be exactly three inches—and declared, "It is a very good height, indeed." Then, without another word, he blew another great cloud of smoke and disappeared inside it.

"But I'm not used to it," Alice wailed, peering into the cloud of smoke. "And you needn't shout," she shouted, puffing out her cheeks and angrily blowing the smoke away.

Alice decided that she had a good deal more to say to the Caterpillar, but she never got a chance. By the time the smoke cleared, the Caterpillar had vanished. All that remained was one big water pipe and six little slippers.

"Oh dear," Alice said, picking up one of the slippers, which she dropped immediately at the sound of a familiar voice overhead.

"By the way," she heard the Caterpillar say, "I have another helpful hint: One side will make you grow taller, and the other side will make you grow shorter."

Alice looked up and saw that the Caterpillar had turned into a butterfly. "One side of what?" she cried as he fluttered by.

"The mushroom, of course," replied the butterfly. And then he was gone.

Chapter Eight

Alice sat on the mushroom, broke off a piece from either side, and wondered which was which. As there was really no way to tell, she simply shrugged her shoulders and bit into one.

The next thing Alice knew, her shoulders were nowhere near where she expected them to be. When she looked down, all she could see was an immense length of neck poking up through the treetops.

Alice had no doubt whatsoever that she had chosen the correct piece of mushroom. But while she searched in vain for her feet—which were far, far below—Alice was suddenly attacked by a mother bird whose nest Alice guessed she must have disturbed. The mother bird took one look at Alice and jumped to the wrong conclusion.

"A serpent!" the mother bird squawked, flapping her wings in Alice's face. "Help! Help! Serpent!"

"But I'm not a serpent," Alice protested.

"Then just what are you?" she demanded, perching on Alice's nose for a closer inspection.

"I'm just a little girl," Alice said.

"Little!" the bird exclaimed. "Little? Ha!"

"Well, I am," said Alice. "I mean, I was. . . ."

"And I suppose you don't eat eggs, either?" asked the mother bird.

"Well, yes, I . . . I do," Alice had to admit, "but—"

"I knew it," cried the mother bird, frantically gathering up her eggs from the nest. "Serrrrpent!" she cawed one last time, and off she flew.

Alice sighed, then decided to bite into the other piece of mushroom and quickly found herself shrinking back down to where she'd started. Or rather, a bit past where she'd started.

"Goodness," Alice said, so tiny now that she stood looking up at a blade of grass. "I wonder if I'll ever get the knack of it."

Then Alice had a thought. She stuck her tongue out and lightly licked the first piece of mushroom. Once again she started to grow, but slowly. And, for a change, she stopped exactly where she wanted to stop.

"There! That's much better," Alice said, pleased to be her normal size again. And tucking both pieces of mushroom into her pocket—just in case—she continued on her way.

Presently, Alice came to a crossroad. As she stood there, wondering which way to go, she could hear someone singing a very strange song.

'Twas brillig, and the slithy toves
    Did gyre and gimble in the wabe;
All mimsy were the borogoves,
    And the mome raths outgrabe.

Alice followed the sound to a big tree, but though she could still hear the song, there was no sign at all of who might be singing. When the music stopped, she slowly circled the tree trunk. "Now where in the world do you suppose . . . ?"

"Lose something?" a voice inquired.

Startled, Alice looked up and, not quite believing her eyes, looked again. There, high up in the tree, between two branches, was a wide, crescent-shaped smile.

"Oh! No . . . I . . . I . . . ," Alice said, quite flustered by the sight. "I mean, I was just wondering."

"That's quite all right," said the smile.

All of a sudden two eyes materialized just above the grin, then two ears, several whiskers, four paws, and finally, a tail. "Second chorus," it announced as it began singing the same silly song once more.

"Why, you're a cat," exclaimed Alice as the whole creature slowly took shape and settled down on a lower branch. "A Cheshire cat," she said more specifically. But no sooner had Alice figured that out than the creature vanished.

"Oh, wait!" Alice cried. "Don't leave!" A moment later the Cheshire Cat reappeared. But before he could start singing again, Alice blurted out, "Thank you, but I just wanted to ask you which way I ought to go."

"That depends on where you want to get to," the Cheshire Cat replied.

"It really doesn't matter," said Alice, "as long as I—"

"Then it really doesn't matter which way you go," he concluded. And once again the cat disappeared.

Alice was beginning to find all this coming and going quite tedious. But while she was sitting, wondering what to do next, the Cheshire Cat appeared yet again.

"If you'd really like to know," he said, pointing one striped paw to the left, "he went that way."

"Who did?" Alice said.

"The White Rabbit," said the Cheshire Cat, as if it were really quite obvious. "If you're looking for him, you'd best ask the Mad Hatter."

"The Mad Hatter!" Alice echoed, not at all sure she liked the sound of that.

"Or, there's the March Hare," the Cheshire Cat said. "But of course he's mad, too."

"But I don't want to go among mad people," wailed Alice.

"Oh, you can't help that. Most everyone's mad here," the Cheshire Cat assured her. "You may have noticed," he went on, "that I'm not all there myself."

Then, beginning with his tail and ending with his grin, the Cheshire Cat slowly began to disappear. But this time, the grin lingered in the air long after the rest of the cat had vanished. Then it, too, was gone.

Chapter Nine

As things turned out, Alice found not only the March Hare but the Mad Hatter as well. The two were sitting at one end of a long, beautifully decorated table, surrounded by a picket fence, in the middle of the woods. They were both drinking tea and having a high old time.

Actually, they were doing a lot more spilling of tea than drinking of it. As they sang and danced about, the Mad Hatter and the March Hare kept sloshing tea all over themselves *and* each other. Only now and then did any tea end up in any of the many little teacups that had been set around the table.

Not wishing to be rude by interrupting, Alice quietly took a seat at the other end of the table and waited for an opportunity to be introduced. All of a sudden the Mad Hatter and the March Hare broke off their singing and, taking notice of Alice, swooped down on her. "No room! No room!" they both cried. "Sorry, all filled up!"

"But there's plenty of room," Alice declared, peering down the length of the big empty table.

"Oh, but it's very rude to sit down without being invited," the March Hare informed Alice.

"I'll say," the Mad Hatter said. "It's very, very rude."

"Very, very, very rude indeed," the Dormouse agreed, popping

his head out of the teapot, where he'd been napping.

"I'm so sorry," Alice apologized, "but I did enjoy your singing, and I—"

"You enjoyed our singing?" chuckled the March Hare.

"Oh, what a delightful child," beamed the Mad Hatter. "You must have some tea."

"That would be nice," Alice said, trying to ignore that the Mad Hatter had just dunked his elbow into a full cup of tea. "I'm sorry I interrupted your birthday party," she added politely.

"Birthday?" the March Hare snorted. "My dear child, this is not a birthday party!"

"This is an unbirthday party!" the Mad Hatter chimed in. When Alice just looked at him blankly, he went on to explain why unbirthdays were so much better than birthdays. With everyone getting just one birthday each year, the March Hare pointed out, that left 364 unbirthdays to celebrate. And that is just what the Mad Hatter and the March Hare were doing.

Alice considered the idea for a moment, then laughed out loud. "Why, then today is my unbirthday, too!" she announced happily.

"It is?" the Mad Hatter said. "What a small world!" Tipping his hat in honor of Alice, he removed from under it a lovely unbirthday cake, which he presented to her with a flourish.

While Alice admired her cake, the Mad Hatter and the March Hare joined hands and danced around her, singing a very merry unbirthday song.

"Now blow out the candle, my dear," said the Mad Hatter.

Alice took a deep breath, made a wish, and blew. *Whoosh!* For a moment the golden flame on the candle sizzled and fizzled. Then, like a rocket, the cake blasted off and zoomed high into the sky.

Alice gasped as a dazzling explosion of fireworks rained down all around her. When she looked up again, she was even more amazed to see the Dormouse floating down to earth. He was hanging on to a blue umbrella and calmly reciting a poem:

Twinkle, twinkle, little bat,
How I wonder what you're at.
Up above the world you fly,
Like a tea tray in the sky!

After the Dormouse had settled back down for a nap in his teapot, the Mad Hatter poured Alice a cup of tea. Before she could take a sip, however, he hollered, "Clean cup! Clean cup!" and yanked Alice up from her chair.

"But I haven't used my cup," Alice protested as the March Hare hustled her down the table, crying, "Move down, move down. Clean cup, clean cup."

As soon as Alice was seated again, the Mad Hatter asked, "Would you like a little more tea?"

"Well, I haven't had *any* yet," Alice pointed out, "so I can't very well take more."

"You mean you can't very well take less," said the March Hare, dumping spoonful after spoonful of sugar into Alice's cup.

"Yes," the Mad Hatter said logically, "you can always take more than nothing."

Alice was busy mulling that puzzle over when the Mad Hatter said kindly, "Something seems to be troubling you, my dear. Won't you tell us all about it?"

"Yes," said the March Hare, hopping up onto the table. "Begin at the beginning."

"Well, it all started while I was sitting on the riverbank with Dinah," Alice explained.

57

"Very interesting," the March Hare commented between sips of tea. "Who's Dinah?"

"Why, Dinah is my cat," Alice said. "You see . . ."

Suddenly the Dormouse popped out of his teapot and shrieked, "C-A-T!

"Cat . . . cat . . . cat . . . cat . . . cat!" the Dormouse howled in alarm. Then he ran off down the table, with the March Hare and the Mad Hatter hot on his heels.

"Oh my goodness!" the March Hare cried, grabbing the Dormouse by the tail and dropping him back into the teapot.

"Quick! Get the jam!" the Mad Hatter yelled at Alice. "Put it on his nose."

Alice, utterly confused, nevertheless did as she was told. She smeared a dollop of jam on his nose, and it seemed to calm the Dormouse down. Before long, he was sleeping soundly. Then the March Hare handed Alice another cup of tea.

But no sooner had Alice raised the cup to her lips than the Mad Hatter snatched it away, crying, "Clean cup!" and "Move down!"

"But I *still* haven't used this one," declared Alice as the March Hare marched her farther down the table.

"And now, my dear, as you were saying?" The Mad Hatter motioned for Alice to continue her story. But the minute she began, he interrupted her again. "Don't you care for tea?" he asked, pouring it straight from the teapot into his mouth.

"Why, yes, I'm very fond of tea," said Alice, who had yet to swallow a sip, "but—"

"If you don't care for tea," the March Hare broke in, "you could at least make polite conversation."

"Well," sputtered Alice, "I've been trying to ask you—"

"I have an excellent idea," the March Hare said. "Let's change the subject. How about a nice cup of tea?" he asked Alice graciously.

59

"A cup of tea, indeed!" snapped Alice, jumping up from the table. "Well, I'm sorry," she said, not at all apologetic, "but I just haven't the time."

"The time, the time! Who's got the time?" the March Hare cried.

Just then the White Rabbit hopped into view. "No, no, no, no time," he muttered. "No time at all. Oh, I'm so late," he said, pulling out his pocketwatch. "So very, very late."

While the White Rabbit continued to fret, the March Hare snatched the pocketwatch out of his paw. "Well, no wonder you're late," he said, shaking the watch and holding it up to his ear. "Why, this clock is exactly two days slow."

"My goodness, we'll have to look into this," the Mad Hatter said, taking the watch from the March Hare and dipping it into his tea. Then he banged it down hard on the table. The watch-case popped open, and the insides spilled out in a tumble.

"Aha!" the Mad Hatter cried, much to the alarm of the White Rabbit. "I see what's wrong. Why, this watch is full of wheels and screws." He flicked the works onto the table with his fork.

"Oh, my poor watch," moaned the Rabbit. "Oh, my wheels and springs," he groaned. "But, but, but . . ."

"Butter!" the Mad Hatter giggled. "Of course! It needs some butter!"

"But, but, butter?" echoed the White Rabbit as the Mad Hatter reached for a knife and began spreading butter all over the watch.

"This is the very best butter," the Mad Hatter assured the White Rabbit, adding another dab or two, just to be safe.

"Tea?" offered the March Hare suddenly. Before the White Rabbit could decline, the March Hare poured a generous splash over the watch.

That made the Mad Hatter think that a bit of sugar might help.

60

But when the sugar didn't work, he reached for the jam.

This time the White Rabbit was quicker. "No, no!" he cried. "Not jam!"

"Mustard?" the March Hare suggested helpfully.

"Don't let's be silly," said the Mad Hatter, picking up a lemon and squirting it over the broken watch. Then he banged the watchcase closed.

"That should do it!" the Mad Hatter said proudly. But then the watch popped open again, and it began bouncing and hopping across the table, bells ringing, springs springing.

"Look!" exclaimed the March Hare. "It's going mad!"

The Mad Hatter shook his head sorrowfully. "I can't understand it," he said. "It was the best butter."

"There's only one way to stop a mad watch," declared the March Hare. He picked up a heavy wooden mallet and brought it down—*smash!*—on the runaway watch.

The White Rabbit took one desparing look at the pile of junk and began to weep. "Oh, my watch . . ."

The Mad Hatter's eyes darted from the rabbit to the watch and back again. "*Your* watch?" he said.

"Yes," the White Rabbit sobbed. "And it was an unbirthday present, too."

"Well, in that case," said the March Hare, "a very merry unbirthday to *you*!" And with no further ado, he and the Mad Hatter grabbed the White Rabbit by all four paws and flung him over the fence.

Chapter Ten

This time Alice didn't even bother to follow the White Rabbit. She'd decided that she'd had quite enough of him—*and* his silly friends.

"I'm going home," Alice announced, turning her back on the tea party. "Straight home." But that, she soon discovered, was easier said than done.

Alice hadn't gone far when she came to a signpost that read Tulgey Wood. "That's curious," she thought. "I don't remember seeing this before." Nor did she remember the odd birds that suddenly flocked around her. There were horn birds, umbrella birds, mirror birds, and even a cage bird. And they were all staring at Alice as if *she* were strange!

"Oh dear," Alice sighed, gazing nervously over her shoulder. It was getting dreadfully dark, and nothing looked familiar.

Alice tried retracing her steps, but that didn't look right, either. As she stood there wondering which way to go, a flock of hammer birds nailed five small boards to the trees. A moment later a pencil bird swooped down and wrote "Don't" on the first board. Then, in quick succession, four more pencil birds wrote "Step," "On," "The," and "Mome Raths" on the other boards.

"Don't—step—on—the—mome raths," Alice read aloud. "*Mome raths?*" she repeated, automatically glancing down at her

feet. And there, springing up from the ground, was a whole army of the little creatures. Alice stared as they banded together in an arrow-shaped formation and began marching deeper into the woods. Since Alice couldn't think of anyplace else to go, she marched after them.

Alice breathed a sigh of relief when the mome raths led her straight to a smoothly laid-out path. "Oh, I just knew I'd find one sooner or later," she cried, running down it. "If I hurry, perhaps I might even be home in time for tea!"

But Alice hadn't gone very far when an unusual-looking dog suddenly appeared and began sweeping the path away. Before long, not a trace remained. With a final proud swish of his tail, the dog trotted off, leaving Alice lost and alone once more. "Oh dear," she sighed. "Now I shall never get out."

Alice sat down wearily on a rock, not at all sure what to do next. Finally, she took a deep breath and said to herself, "Well, when one is lost, I suppose it's good advice to stay where you are until someone finds you." But immediately she thought, Who would ever think to look for me here?

Alice tried hard to be brave, but she couldn't stop the tears that welled up in her eyes. And when a puffy cloud drifted across the moon and turned the sky black, Alice bowed her head and wept.

When Alice finally raised her head again, the first thing she saw was a shining crescent overhead. At first she thought it was the moon. But she quickly realized her mistake.

"Oh, it's you, Cheshire Cat," said Alice as the smiling creature took shape on a branch high in a tree.

"Whom did you expect?" he asked. "The White Rabbit?"

"Oh, no, no, no. I'm through with rabbits," Alice declared. "I just want to go home," she said wistfully, "but I can't find my way."

"That's because you have no way," the Cheshire Cat pointed out. "All ways here are the Queen's ways."

Not for the first time, Alice realized that she had no idea what the Cheshire Cat was talking about. "What Queen?" Alice asked. "I've never met any Queen."

"You haven't?" cried the Cheshire Cat. "Oh, but you must! She'll be mad about you . . . simply *mad*!" The Cheshire Cat giggled wildly.

"Please," Alice said seriously, "how can I find her?"

"Well, some go this way," the Cheshire Cat said, pointing one way. "And some go that way," he said, pointing the other way. "But as for me, myself, personally," he said, "I prefer the shortcut."

And with that, the cat reached up and pulled on the branch above his head. Then, slowly and smoothly, a secret door in the tree trunk swung open.

Without a second thought, Alice walked through the door.

67

Chapter Eleven

Alice emerged into a beautiful garden. She blinked her eyes against the glare of the sun, then blinked again to be sure that what she *thought* she was seeing was *really* what she was seeing.

As far as Alice could tell, three very peculiar-looking gardeners were tending a bower of white roses. The gardeners looked just like playing cards except that they had arms and legs. And instead of rakes and hoes, as Alice might have expected, they were carrying paintbrushes and buckets.

Alice walked over to the Three of Clubs, who was perched on a ladder, frantically splashing red paint all over the beautiful white blossoms.

"Oh, pardon me, Mister Three," she said, "but what are you doing?"

The gardener stopped his work just long enough to lean down and whisper into Alice's ear. "We're painting the roses red," he said nervously. "The fact is, miss, we planted the white roses by mistake, and the Queen likes them red. If she knew what we'd done, we'd all lose our heads."

"Oh dear!" said Alice, picking up a brush and joining the Ace and the Deuce of Clubs, who were hard at work on another rosebush. "Do let me help you."

Alice was just putting the finishing touches on the last rose when a royal fanfare echoed through the garden.

"The Queen!" cried the Three of Clubs, jumping down from his ladder.

"The Queen!" cried the Deuce of Clubs, dropping his bucket.

"The Queen!" cried the Ace of Clubs, hurling his paintbrush over the hedge.

And then, as an army of card guards marched into the garden and lined up in two long columns, all three gardeners threw themselves facedown on the ground. After a puzzled moment's hesitation Alice dropped down beside them, too. And, as it turned out, not a moment too soon.

There was another fanfare, and the White Rabbit came hopping down the center of the columns, trumpet in hand. "Her Imperial Highness!" he announced breathlessly. "Her Grace! Her Excellency! Her Royal Majesty . . . the Queen of Hearts!"

The Queen was greeted by loud cheers as she made her grand entrance.

"And the King!" added the White Rabbit, only after His Majesty stepped out from behind the Queen's skirt and tapped him meaningfully on the shoulder.

"Hurray," a lone voice called out.

As the Queen's sharp eye searched out the culprit, her royal gaze fell on a rosebush whose wet petals were glistening in the sun. With her royal finger, she flicked a drop of red paint from a snow white petal. The Queen sniffed the rose suspiciously. "Who dares to taint a royal rose with vulgar paint?" she shouted.

When no one stepped forward, she stomped over to the three terrified gardeners. "Someone will lose his head for this," the Queen threatened.

"It's all Two's fault," the Three of Clubs lifted his head to say.

70

"Not me, Your Grace," the Two of Clubs protested. "It was the Ace."

"You?" the Queen demanded of the Ace.

"No, Two," he replied, even as the Two pointed an accusing finger at the Three.

"That's enough!" yelled the Queen. Turning to her guards, she cried, "Off with their heads. All of them."

"Oh, please!" said Alice as the three gardeners were dragged away. "They were only trying to—"

"And who is this?" demanded the Queen, looking down at Alice.

"Well, well, well," mumbled the King. "Now let me see, my dear. It certainly isn't a heart," he deduced. "Perhaps it's a club?"

The Queen gave the King a withering glance, then peered into Alice's face. "Why, it's a little girl," she said after a thorough inspection.

"Yes," Alice said softly, "and I was hoping—"

"Look up, speak nicely, and don't twiddle your fingers," the Queen said sharply. "Turn out your toes," she commanded. "Curtsey, open your mouth a little wider, and always," she concluded, "say, 'Yes, Your Majesty!' "

Alice took a deep breath, turned out her toes, and made a pretty curtsey. Then she opened her mouth wide and said nicely, "Yes, Your Majesty," with scarcely a twiddle at all.

The Queen smiled approvingly at Alice and patted her on the head. "Now, where do you come from," she asked, "and where are you going?"

"Well," Alice replied sadly, "I'm trying to find my way home."

The Queen's smile faded from her royal face. "*Your* way," she roared. "All ways here are *my* ways." The "my" was said with such force that Alice was actually knocked off her feet.

"Y-yes, I-I know," Alice stammered. "But I was just thinking—"

"Curtsey while you're thinking," said the Queen imperiously. "It saves time."

"Yes, Your Majesty," Alice said, doing her best to curtsey while sprawled on the ground. "I was only going to ask—"

"*I'll* ask the questions," the Queen informed her. "Do you play croquet?" she asked Alice quite out of the blue.

"Why, y-yes, Your Majesty," Alice replied uncertainly.

Apparently that was the right answer, for the Queen graced Alice with a royal smile, took her by the hand, and enthusiastically declared, "Then let the game begin!"

Chapter Twelve

Though Alice had indeed played croquet before, she'd never played anything quite like the Queen's version.

For one thing, the mallets were flamingos, the balls were hedgehogs, and the wickets were playing cards. For another, it seemed that the whole purpose of the game was to make sure the Queen won.

When the Queen struck a hedgehog with her flamingo, all the cards scurried into position. The hedgehog had nothing to do but roll right on through. And even when the Queen took a wild swing and missed the wicket entirely, the hedgehog would change direction and roll obligingly straight for the equally obliging wickets, who scrambled hurriedly to line up in exactly the right place at exactly the right time.

When Alice's turn came, however, neither the ball nor the wicket were nearly as obliging. Her flamingo wasn't the least bit cooperative. It not only refused to act like a mallet, it had the nerve to grab Alice by the ankles and take a swing with *her*!

Alice finally wrestled her flamingo into the proper position and even managed to hit her hedgehog. As the hedgehog went barreling down the lawn, though, the cards hurried out of its path. Alice's hedgehog rolled straight into a tree without passing through a single wicket.

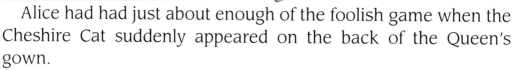

Alice had had just about enough of the foolish game when the Cheshire Cat suddenly appeared on the back of the Queen's gown.

"I say," said the Cheshire Cat, "how are you getting on?"

"Not at all!" Alice replied emphatically.

"Who are you talking to?" the Queen asked just as the smiling cat disappeared from her bustle and reappeared on her shoulder.

"Oh . . . a . . . a . . . cat, Your Majesty," Alice stammered.

"Cat?" the Queen echoed. "Where?"

"There!" said Alice, pointing to the Queen's shoulder. But by the time the Queen turned her head, the Cheshire Cat was gone again.

"Oh-h-h!" Alice cried as the Cheshire Cat reappeared on the Queen's royal bustle. "There he is again."

But the Queen, of course, saw nothing. "I warn you, child," she said, "if I lose my temper, you lose your head. Understand?"

Alice, who understood quite well, nodded her head gravely. But the Cheshire Cat only widened his grin and whispered to Alice, "We could make her really angry. Shall we try?"

"Oh, no!" cried Alice, horrified at the thought.

"But it's loads of fun," said the Cheshire Cat. Before Alice could utter a word, however, the cat reached down and hooked the flamingo's beak under the Queen's hem.

When the Queen swung her flamingo, instead of the ball it was her skirt that went flying—right over her head.

"Oh, my fur and whiskers!" mumbled the White Rabbit at the sight of the Queen's royal knickers.

The royal guard quickly surrounded the Queen, and it wasn't long before she'd regained her feet. But the Queen was furious.

"Someone's head will roll for this!" she shouted. Her angry glare swept over the crowd and came to rest on Alice. "Yours!" she roared.

Alice backed away fearfully, toppling a column of cards, but there was no escape. "Off with her head!" the Queen cried.

The guards were already closing in on Alice when the King spoke up on her behalf. "Couldn't she have a trial first?" he asked the Queen. "Hmm?"

"Trial?" bellowed the Queen.

"Well . . . uh . . . just a little trial?" suggested the King timidly. "Hmm?"

The Queen considered his suggestion for a moment, then nodded agreeably. "Very well," she said, patting the King on the head. "Let the trial begin!"

Chapter Thirteen

Alice was waiting nervously in the prisoner's dock when the White Rabbit entered the courtroom and blew a royal fanfare on his trumpet. When he had everyone's attention, he held up an official scroll and began to read: "Your Majesty, members of the jury, loyal subjects—"

"Ahem!" the King piped up.

"—and the King," added the White Rabbit. "The prisoner at the bar is charged with enticing Her Majesty, the Queen of Hearts, into a game of croquet, thereby willfully and with malice afore-thought teasing, tormenting, and otherwise annoying our beloved and—"

"Never mind all that," the Queen said impatiently. "Get to the part where I lose my temper!"

"Thereby causing the Queen to lose her temper!" the White Rabbit wisely concluded.

The Queen smiled sweetly at the White Rabbit, then turned to Alice. "Are you ready for your sentence?" she asked Alice gravely.

"Sentence?" Alice gulped. "Oh, but there must be a verdict first."

"Sentence first! Verdict afterward!" the Queen insisted. "Off with her head!"

"But we've called no witnesses, my dear," the King pointed

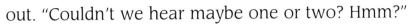

out. "Couldn't we hear maybe one or two? Hmm?"

"Oh, very well," the Queen agreed, "but get on with it!"

And before she could change her mind, the King said to the White Rabbit, "Herald, call the first witness."

"The March Hare," the White Rabbit called out.

The March Hare entered the courtroom carrying a cup and saucer.

"Now," the King said as soon as the March Hare was settled in the witness box, "what do you know about this unfortunate affair?"

The March Hare thoughtfully stirred his tea with his finger. "Nothing," he said finally.

"Nothing whatever?" asked the Queen.

"Nothing whatever!" said the March Hare.

"That's very important! Jury, write that down!" the Queen commanded.

The next witness was the Dormouse, who was brought to the witness box in his teapot. "Well, what have you to say about all this?" the Queen asked.

The Dormouse replied:

Twinkle, twinkle, little bat,
How I wonder—

"That's the most important piece of evidence we've heard yet!" the Queen said, cutting him off. "Jury, write that down."

The final witness was the Mad Hatter. No sooner had he sat down, though, than the Queen screamed, "Off with your hat!"

The Mad Hatter respectfully removed his hat. And under the hat was a teapot. But as the Queen had no objection to the teapot on the Mad Hatter's head, the King began his questioning of the witness.

81

"Where were you when the horrible crime was committed?" he asked.

"I was home drinking tea," replied the Mad Hatter. "Today is my unbirthday."

"Why, today is *your* unbirthday, too, my dear," the King said, turning to the Queen.

"It is?" she exclaimed happily.

"It is?" the March Hare and Mad Hatter chorused. And then, of course, there was nothing to be done but for all of them to sing a royal rendition of the unbirthday song and present the Queen with an unbirthday cake.

The Queen had just blown out the candles when the Cheshire Cat appeared on top of her crown.

"Oh, Your Majesty," Alice cried out suddenly.

"Yes, my dear?" said the Queen, still aglow with unbirthday cheer.

"Look! There he is now," said Alice.

"Who? Where?" said the Queen, looking first this way, then that way.

"The Cheshire Cat!" said Alice, pointing to her head.

"Cat?" said the Queen.

"C-A-T! Cat! Cat! Cat! Cat!" howled the Dormouse, and off he ran.

"There he goes!" cried the March Hare, taking off after him.

"Oh, this is terrible!" said the Mad Hatter, joining the chase.

"Stop him!" yelled the March Hare.

"Get me the jam!" yelled the Mad Hatter. "The jam!"

"The jam!" yelled the King. "By order of the King!" Alice helpfully grabbed a jar that just happened to be sitting there, right in front of her.

The March Hare was just dipping a spoon into the jam when

the Queen suddenly hollered, "Let me have it!"

And so he did—*splat!*—right in her royal face!

When the Dormouse scampered over the fallen Queen, the King raised his gavel and brought it down—*thunk!*—right on Her Majesty's royal head.

But before the Queen knew who—or what—had hit her, the King passed the offending gavel to the March Hare, who quickly passed it to the Mad Hatter, who just as quickly passed it to Alice.

"Somebody's head will roll for this!" roared the Queen. She searched the crowd for an acceptable candidate, and she didn't have far to look. For there stood Alice, jam jar in one hand, gavel in the other, a guilty smile on her face.

Alice quickly dropped the jam jar and the gavel and shoved both hands into her pockets. And that's when she discovered the two pieces of mushroom she'd placed there earlier. In desperation, Alice crammed both pieces into her mouth and gulped them down.

"Off with her head!" the Queen cried a split second later. But by then Alice's head was no longer where it had been. With one little bite of mushroom, she had grown into a giant.

With her head in the clouds, Alice looked down, down, down at the guards. "Oh, pooh," she said, and laughed. "I'm not afraid of you. Why, you're nothing but a pack of cards." She gleefully shuffled the whole deck of cards and sent them flying.

The King dashed behind the judge's bench to consult his rule book. "Rule forty-two," he read aloud. "Persons more than a mile high must leave the court immediately!"

"I am not a mile high," Alice informed him, "and I'm not leaving."

"Sorry!" the Queen chimed in, not sounding the slightest bit sorry. "Rule forty-two, you know."

Alice, however, was not impressed. Stooping down over the Queen, she said, "As for you, Your Majesty—

"Your Majesty, indeed," Alice interrupted herself. "Why, you're not a queen. You're just a fat, pompous, bad-tempered old tyrant!"

Even as she spoke, however, Alice could feel herself shrinking. By the time she finished shrinking, she was as small as she'd ever been. Suddenly it was the Queen who was looking down on *her*.

"What were you saying, my dear?" the Queen asked in an ominous voice.

"She simply said that you're a fat, pompous, bad-tempered old tyrant!" said the Cheshire Cat, making another brief appearance atop the Queen's crown. Since that's just what the Queen thought Alice had said, she turned to her guards and screamed, "Off with her head!"

Alice ran for her life, with the whole pack of cards running after her. Behind them came the Queen. "Off with her head!" she cried. And behind her ran the King.

Alice raced through the garden so fast her feet barely touched the ground. In no time at all she found herself back on the beach, where the Dodo's friends were still running around in circles. This time, however, Alice refused to join them. Nor did she accept the Mad Hatter's invitation to tea when she bumped into him and the March Hare a moment later. Even when the Butterfly popped up out of nowhere and asked, "Whoooo are you?" she barely slowed her pace.

In fact, Alice didn't stop running until she came upon the tiny door with the tiny brass doorknob. With the Queen's cries of "Off with her head!" still echoing in the distance, Alice reached out and twisted the knob.

"Ouch!" yelped the Doorknob, wiggling his nose painfully. "Still locked, you know!"

"But the Queen!" Alice cried. "I simply must get out!"

"But you *are* out," said the Doorknob, opening his keyhole wide. "See for yourself."

Alice bent down, put her eye to the opening, and gasped in amazement. For there, on the other side of the door, she could see herself quite plainly. She was lying beneath a shady tree, her cat, Dinah, curled up in her lap.

"Why, that's me," Alice exclaimed. "I'm asleep!"

Of all the strange things she had seen in this strange land, this seemed to be the strangest. But Alice had no time to wonder about it. She could hear the Queen's guards closing in on her.

Alice took one quick look over her shoulder, then turned back to the keyhole. "Alice, wake up!" she shouted to the sleeping girl beneath the tree. "Please wake up, Alice!"

Chapter Fourteen

"Alice! Alice! Alice!"

Alice awoke to the sound of her sister's voice. "Alice, will you kindly pay attention and recite your lesson!"

"Huh?" Alice rubbed her eyes sleepily, then came awake with a start. Jumping to her feet, she curtsied quickly and recited:

How doth the little crocodile
  Improve his shining tail,
And pour the waters of the—

"Alice! What *are* you talking about?" said her sister impatiently.

"Oh, I'm sorry," said Alice. "But you see, the Caterpillar said—"

"Caterpillar!" snorted her sister. "Oh, for goodness' sake!" And when Alice just stood there, looking confused, her sister simply shrugged her shoulders. "Well," she told Alice resignedly, "do come along. It's time for tea."

That sounded like a fine idea to Alice, who suddenly felt quite thirsty. So she bent down, picked up her cat, and followed her sister home.